Baby Penguins Love Their Mama!

This book is for Zoe, Zach,

Zack, Lucas, Paige,

& Holly.

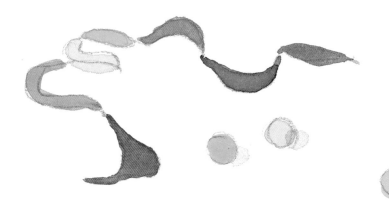

Baby Penguins Love Their Mama!

Melissa Guion

PHILOMEL BOOKS An Imprint of Penguin Group (USA)

Once there was a family of penguins.

A mama penguin . . .

and lots and lots
of baby penguins.

Mama Penguin was very busy
taking care of everybody.

There were swimming
lessons on Monday.

Sliding lessons
on Tuesday.

And waddling on
Wednesday.

Waddling was harder
than it looked.

Thursday was preening practice.
Nobody liked preening practice.

Friday was fishing.

Fishing was fun!

And everyone loved
Saturday squawking!

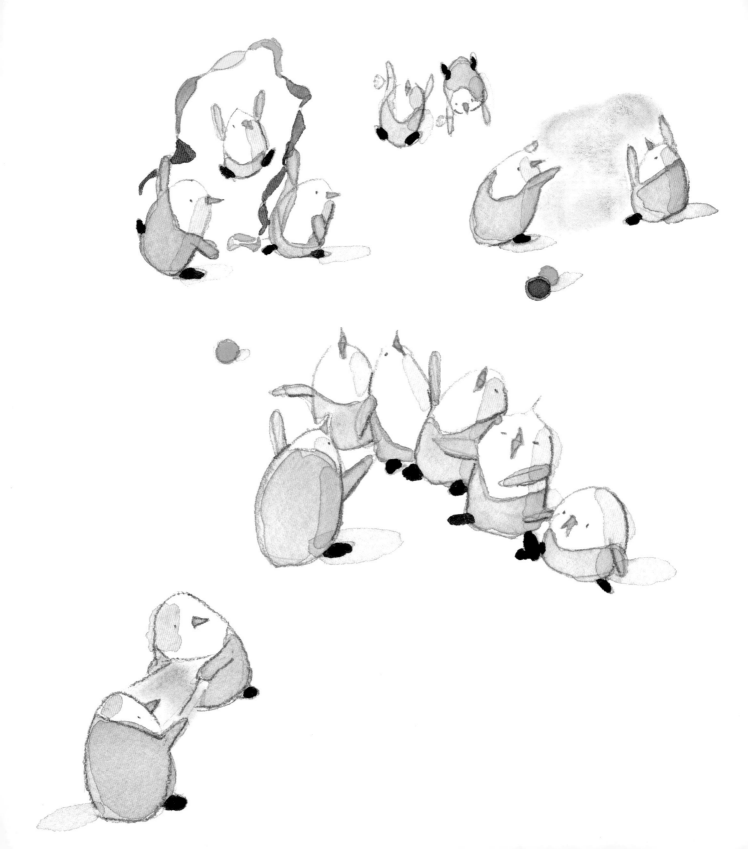

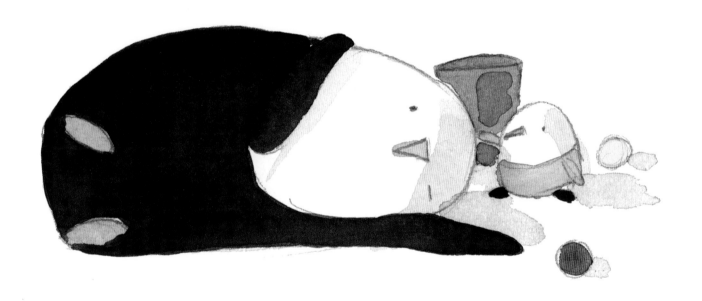

On Sunday, after a long
week, Mama took a nap.

She loved doing all she could
for her babies. And she was
proud of them.

"Soon you will swim and slide, and waddle and preen, and fish and squawk, just as well as I can," she told them.

"Maybe even better,"
said one of the babies.

"Better?" said Mama.

"And when you can do everything better than I can, what will I do?"

"Silly Mama . . ."

"... you will be our Mama!"

PHILOMEL BOOKS
Published by the Penguin Group
Penguin Group (USA) LLC
375 Hudson Street, New York, NY 10014

USA | Canada | UK | Ireland | Australia | New Zealand | India | South Africa | China
penguin.com
A Penguin Random House Company

Library of Congress Cataloging-in-Publication Data
Guion, Melissa.   Baby penguins love their mama! / Melissa Guion.   pages cm
Summary: A mother penguin stays very busy taking care of her many babies and teaching them important
lessons about such things as sliding, waddling, preening—and love.
[1. Penguins—Fiction. 2. Animals—Infancy—Fiction. 3. Parent and child—Fiction.] I. Title.
PZ7.G9434Bal 2014   [E]—dc23   2013015911   Manufactured in China by South China Printing Co. Ltd.
ISBN 978-0-399-16365-4
1 3 5 7 9 10 8 6 4 2

Edited by Michael Green.   Design by Semadar Megged.
Text set in 22-point Veronika.   The illustrations are rendered in watercolor and pencil.